Wild
Daisies

Wild Daisies

the best of
Bub Bridger

with an introduction by
Andrew Mason

MALLINSON RENDEL

Published in 2005
by Mallinson Rendel Publishers Ltd,
PO Box 9409, Wellington
Published in association with Poutama Press,
18 Richmond Road, Mahina Bay, Wellington

National Library of New Zealand
Cataloguing-in-Publication Data
Bridger, Bub.
Wild Daisies: the best of Bub Bridger / by Bub Bridger.
ISBN 0-908783-97-3
I.Title.
NZ821.2 — dc 22

Cover design by Hamish Thompson
Designed and typeset by Anna Brown
Printed and bound through Colorcraft, Hong Kong

ARTS COUNCIL OF NEW ZEALAND *Toi AOTEAROA*

We gratefully acknowledge the assistance
of Creative New Zealand with this publication.

for Shannagh

Contents

* *poems featured on CD*

Introduction

Bub Bridger is a national treasure. She is probably
best known now for her fantasy poems — those
salacious tributes to young men like 'Ode to Jokers' and
'A Christmas Wish' which, delivered with an enticing
blend of lust and wistfulness by this white-haired old
lady wearing reading glasses, can have audiences in
tears of laughter. But there is much more to Bub Bridger
than that. First there was the writer of often poignant,
sometimes savage, short stories. Then came the writer of
shorter poems that glow with feeling and delight in being
alive. This book is a selection of her most captivating
work in all three genres, and comes with a CD of Bub
reading some of her best-loved performance pieces.

Bub Bridger is of Maori (Ngati Kahungunu) and Irish
ancestry — two cultures that celebrate the spoken word.
She was born and raised in Napier, working in a hat
factory and tobacco factory there after leaving high
school at the age of fourteen. She came to Wellington
while still a teenager to work in the old Social Security
Department (now Work and Income New Zealand).
She married and had four children, but soon fled the
marriage, taking the children with her. Hard times
followed. But Bub had been a voracious reader as a girl

and hoped that, once her children were grown up, she could at last pursue her interest in writing.

In 1974 she attended a creative writing course run by Michael King at Victoria University. This was the start she needed: 'Michael was the one who showed me the way. When he read my first short story he said, "You are going to be a writer."' He was right, of course. Bub's first story, 'The Stallion', was published in the *Listener* the next year. But she has never been a prolific writer of short stories – fewer than ten in all, written over a dozen years. They have since been anthologised many times in Maori, New Zealand and even international collections, and almost all appear in this selection. The power of these stories lies in their apparent simplicity. The narrator is often a young girl, and Bub deftly captures not only the thoughts but the thought patterns of her main characters. Beneath the smooth flow of the narrative we sense real people with real and complex and conflicting emotions. It is an art that conceals its art.

The same is true of her poetry. After a visit to Ireland and the home of her father in 1984, she wrote her very first poem, a short tribute to him. This too was published in the *Listener* — and later prompted the much longer 'Johnny Come Dancing', which appears in this selection. After this there was no stopping her: 'I started to think poetry. It was the most incredible experience. I came home to New Zealand and I couldn't get it down fast enough.' All the poems that followed appeared in the *Listener* until it stopped publishing poetry for a time in the 1990s. As the magazine's literary editor in the 1980s, I used to dread it when Bub's poems appeared because they attracted so many imitations, none of which came anywhere near the quality of her work. Again, it's the art that conceals art. Bub writes so lightly about the things that matter so deeply to all of us — love and hope and beauty, sadness and pain and loss. These feelings are at the heart of life, and Bub gets to the heart of them — and all in a handful of words.

A collection of her poetry, *Up Here on the Hill*, appeared in 1989. About the same time, the Hens' Teeth collective of women performing artists asked her to join them to read some of her poems. Out of that grew those deliberately risqué poems celebrating men, and a whole new career as a performing artist for Bub. The most famous of these fantasy poems is undoubtedly 'A Christmas Wish'. Her wantonly expressed desire for the All Black Whetton brothers created a national enthusiasm for the work of this 'elderly maker of rhyme' — and also led ultimately to the present selection. Despite many requests, Bub has always resisted publishing these poems, feeling that her tongue-in-cheek delivery is an integral part of them and fearing that on the printed page they would give people the wrong impression about her. After Bub celebrated her eightieth birthday, it was possible to persuade her to publish and record these classic pieces. From that grew the idea of a selection of *all* her best work, poems and stories.

In all her writing, Bub Bridger is 100 percent honest with the reader. She opens up her heart and tells us exactly how she felt, whether good or bad, in the simplest of words. She can laugh at herself and make us laugh with her. She can make us feel her joy and excitement, her sorrow and grief — and her defiance of pain. It is a privilege to be taken into her life and her heart in the words that follow.

Andrew Mason

Wild Daisies

If you love me
Bring me flowers
Wild daisies
Clutched in your fist
Like a torch
No orchids or roses
Or carnations
No florist's bow
Just daisies
Steal them
Risk your life for them
Up the sharp hills
In the teeth of the wind
If you love me
Bring me daisies
Wild daisies
That I will cram
In a bright vase
And marvel at

Thirteenth Summer

When Tyrone Power got married I was going to kill myself. I was twelve years old, we had never met, and he was thousands of miles away, but my passion knew no rules or boundaries. I had seen all his films, and I made a scrap-book out of brown wrapping paper where I carefully pasted every cut-out picture and Hollywood gossip item I could find.

Until he got married.

There it was on the *Daily Telegraph* film page:

TYRONE POWER WEDS FRENCH STAR, ANNABELLA.

The shock made my breath stop and my ears roar. I almost fainted.

How could he? How could he? I went outside and pressed my face against the rough bricks of the chimney.

'Oh, God,' I moaned. 'I'm going to kill myself!'

Nobody heard me. Nobody cared. And there was no one I could turn to. No one I could open my heart to. I would just have to be very secretive about it and then go away somewhere and die. Of a broken heart.

My mother came round the corner of the house.

'What's wrong with you?' she asked, bristling and suspicious. 'Are you mooning over boys, again?'

I wasn't allowed to moon over boys.

I couldn't tell her. I could never tell her anything. She didn't understand me and she certainly wouldn't understand about Tyrone Power. She had never seen *In Old Chicago* or *Suez*. She liked Clark Gable.

'There's nothing wrong with me,' I said. But inside, my bleeding heart threatened to burst through my ribs. I wished it would. That would show her. I would lie there dying, and how overcome with grief and guilt she would be. I wouldn't forgive her. I would turn away from her and close my eyes forever. But my broken heart kept right on beating . . .

'Is it that other business?'

'No,' I said.

'Well, stop acting like a dying calf!' Her dark eyes shone with dislike.

I went running through the garden and raced away down through the orchard to the creek.

'You bitch!' I whispered. 'You bitch! You bitch! You bitch!'

I took all my clothes off and sat down in the water. It was cold and clean, and it flowed round me and down over my legs like balm. Then I noticed red swirls that paled to ribbony pink, in the water between my legs.

'Oh, Jesus!' I said. 'It is that other business.'

I couldn't think of a way to die. Throwing myself under a moving train would do it, or leaping off some high cliff, or a bullet through my brain, but there were complications. We lived a very long way from a railway station, and there weren't any cliffs around, only the smooth rolling hills across the plain. Uncle Tom Harrow owned a gun, the only one I'd ever seen, but it was too huge for me to handle. Also, I wasn't quite sure where my brain was. Alas! There was no way I could kill myself. I would just have to waste away. I wrote poems in the back of my school exercise books about heartbreak and about dying for love. They were so beautiful that I cried when I read them. I pinned a copy of the saddest one to my singlet every morning when I got dressed. Just above my heart. It was very comforting.

But after a week I couldn't keep it to myself any longer.

Walking home from school with Sadie Cooper, who was sometimes my best friend, I put out a feeler.

'Sadie, did you read last Friday's film page?'

'No,' said Sadie.

'Oh,' I said, 'there was a bit about Tyrone Power in it. He got married.'

'Did he?' said Sadie.

'Yes — to Annabella.'

'Who?'

'Annabella.'

'Annabella who?'

I sighed.

'She doesn't have another name. She's a film star. She's French. And very famous. She was in *Suez*.'

'Oh,' said Sadie, 'I don't go to the pictures much.'

'But you've seen Tyrone Power?'

'Oh, yes, I've seen him. I think. Was there a picture of him in the *Home Journal*?'

'Fancy not knowing whether or not you've seen Tyrone Power,' I marvelled. 'Sadie, do you know what? A whole class in a girls' school in America put black bands around their arms and cried for days when he got married.'

'How do you know?'

'I read it. It was in the Friday film page.'

'Why did they do that?'

'Because they were so sad.'

Sadie shrugged.

'He's only a film star,' she said.

'Oh, yes, I know!' I said quickly. 'But don't you feel a bit sad?'

'No,' said Sadie.

We walked on in silence. It was very hot and the road was long and dusty.

'I wish I had a bike,' said Sadie.

'So do I,' I sighed.

When I got home there was nobody there and I went off down to the creek. I gathered stones in the lap of my skirt and carried them up to the bare ground under the walnut tree at the end of the orchard. Then I went back and got some more. I drew a square in the soil and filled it in with the stones and before it I wrote TYRONE in pebbles. It looked quite beautiful. A little shrine to my love embedded in the sour earth where nothing grew.

'I love you,' I whispered, 'but you have betrayed me.'

I lay there on the ground with my cheek pressed to the dirt, dry-eyed, and desolate.

'I'll come here every day after school,' I vowed, 'and I'll

put another pebble on the shrine. And as it grows, I'll get sicker and sicker!'

The next day after school, I found the shrine flattened and the inscription gone. There was a message spelled out with the stones. YOU ARE MAD. I froze with shock. Who would do that?

On the way to school the next day, I questioned Sadie. 'Someone wrote "YOU ARE MAD" under our big walnut tree with some stones I had there.'

'Did they?'

'Sadie, was it you?'

'What?'

'Did you break my shrine?'

Sadie frowned. 'What's a shrine?'

I shrugged. 'Never mind.'

So I carried all the stones back to the creek. The sun shone and the water sparkled, the sky was silver and the leaves of the tall poplar tree that marked our boundary shimmered in the summer air. I took off all my clothes and lay down in the water. The creek carried me down past the pebbly shallows into deeper water and I turned into a fish. It was a big surprise. I usually turned into a fish only when I was very happy, but here I was, being a fish, finned and tailed and glittering, when my whole life had been shattered. Twisting, darting, turning somersaults and blowing bubbles, I couldn't stop. I went skimming along all the way to the culvert that went under the road. But that stopped me. There were eels in the culvert as thick as a man's thigh and I turned in terror, fleeing back to the shallows, gasping and shaken, and safe. Suddenly I stopped being a fish. I stood up and ran splashing and screaming and laughing through the water. And I knew I wasn't going to die for Tyrone Power. Or anyone else. I was going to live to be a hundred. Maybe a hundred-and-one! I felt light as a feather.

There was only one thing to do. I climbed out of the creek and got the poem from my singlet. I felt a little bit guilty as I tore it into tiny shreds and let them fall into the water and swirl away. Then I got back into the creek. Tyrone Power's face washed out of my heart and sailed off with the torn scraps of paper to the culvert.

I turned into a fish again and swam and splashed and shimmered in the sun until I heard Uncle Tom Harrow calling the cows.

My mother! 'Oh God, save me from her! I've been here for hours! She'll murder me!'

I hurtled into my clothes and flew back through the orchard to the house, wet and breathless.

'Where've you been till this time?' she blazed.

'Swimming in the creek,' I panted.

She gave me a great clout across the ear, but I scarcely felt it.

I smiled at her.

'I'll peel the potatoes and set the table,' I said.

Men

I must make a confession
I've a wicked obsession
For long-legged, sexy young men.
I try to write words
About flowers and birds
But I've lost all control of my pen.

Ah! Men!

I'm mad about them
Though I've tried to be good
And I know that I should
I just never could
'Cos I'm mad about men.

And I'm glad about men
I just love the way
They lead me astray
And I'm happy to play
'Cos I'm mad about them.

And I'm bad about men
I pretend that I'm sweet
But when I feel the heat
I'll season the meat
'Cos I'm mad about men.

But

I'm scared about men
'Cos now that I'm old
Will passion turn cold?
Indifference take hold?
Oh! I'm sad about men . . .

Na-a-a-ah

I'm mad about them!
And this lust will blaze
In the wickedest ways
Till the end of my days
'Cos I'm mad about men.

To Perth by Rail

Ivy died this morning
There was ice in the wind
Down there it had snowed all night
And I could see the mountains
Rising up out of the sea
Like white castles

Forty-three years ago
I saw her for the first time
Walking up Willis Street
Pushing a pram as big
As herself and laughing down
At her sister's baby —
She was seventeen years old

The other day we spoke
Of my problems my joys
And she told me she
Was planning a trip
From Sydney to Perth by rail
To see her twin sister
But she died this morning

Without fear or fuss
She slipped away sooner
Than she had planned
Or I had expected —

Bon voyage my friend
You'll be well on your way
Riding in the sun to Perth
By rail
Free of the pain now
And in from the cold

Enigma

I can't understand
People
Who don't like dogs
Make prisoners
Of birds in
Cages
Keep the curtains
Drawn
Against the sun
And stay bleak
In marriages
Where only anger
Relieves
The boredom and only
Bitterness
Feeds the soul

Johnny Come Dancing

to Long John Montgomery

1
On Douglas* Bridge
On Douglas Bridge
They were dancing! Dancing!
And he seventeen swinging home
Through the twilight
A day's work done
And not a care in his head
Stopping in wonder
What dancing! Dancing!
Their black curls bouncing
And their red shoes flashing
Five little girls — dancing! Dancing!
With their dark eyes gleaming
And their green dresses shining
Saying — Dance Johnny! Dance!
And we'll give you a shilling!
And he danced and he danced
And he danced till the dawning
Then they were gone
With the grey of the morning
And Johnny limped home
Clutching a shilling
And his mother cried out

* *pronounced 'Dooglies'*

And covered her head
Oh! Johnny my darling
You were not in your bed
And the fairies were out
On Douglas Bridge
Did you dance with them Johnny?
Did they give you a penny?
When he showed her the shilling
She kissed him goodbye
Then she wrapped him a loaf
And a coat for the weather
And that was the last
They were ever together.

2
He wept and he cursed
And he called to his mother
But the five little girls
Dragged him down to the river
Then he begged and he pleaded
That they take back their shilling
But they shook their dark heads
— It's no good your crying
You danced for our shilling
Now you'll dance till you're dying
You'll dance down the road
And you'll dance to the sea
And you'll dance till you reach
The last country
But it won't all be sorrow

Though you'll always be lonely
And you'll weep when you hear
The wild north wind calling
Then they jumped in the river
And when he looked over
There was only a swirl
And the sound of their laughter.

3
So he walked to Lough Foyle
And he met a sea captain
One man short
To sail for New Zealand
Where's that? asked Johnny
Is it far far away?
It's further than that
And we sail in the morning
I'll come then said Johnny
There's nothing to stop me
If I turn back now
The wee folk will get me
And I'll drown in the river
Below Douglas Bridge
And I'll always be cold
And I'll never be resting
For the five little girls
Will be dancing and leaping
And my dear dear mother
By the bridge there weeping.

4

So he sailed for New Zealand
On the outgoing tide
And it wasn't all pain
And it wasn't all grieving
Just so long
As he kept on dancing
And the new land was almost
As green as Ireland
And he married a girl
With her black hair waving
And she led him a dance
And she sneered at his pining
For a two-roomed cottage
With a rammed earth floor
And nothing to keep
The wolf from the door
And she scoffed at his stories
Of little girls dancing
With their black curls bouncing
And their red shoes flashing
But she stopped when she saw
His quick feet flying
For where had she ever
Seen such dancing! Dancing!
With his long legs weaving
And his blue eyes sparkling.

5

So he danced through the years
Through the love and the hating
Through the birth of his children
And her final betrayal
And he danced to his death
One mild spring evening
And he called out her name
As he fell to the floor
And the five little girls
Came through the door
And as he lay dying
He saw so clearly
They all had her face
And her black hair waving
With their dark eyes gleaming
And their green dresses shining
And the very last thing
That he ever saw
Was her dancing . . . dancing . . .
. . . dancing.

Coming Back Down to Earth

for Ry Cooder

Restless
At three a.m.
I turn on the radio
And there you are playing
Guitar like no one else
Filling my heart
Waking me up
Completely and making me
Say thank you to
Whatever it was
That kept me from sleep
And in the morning
I go to town
To buy your music
Everything I can find
Never mind
The rent
Or the phone bill

. . . back home
I play it all day
I sing
With you
To you

As I clean the house
I tell you
I love you and dance
Through all the rooms
Until
In the long mirror
Beside my bed
I see me whirling
Wide-eyed
Flushed
Ecstatic
Joyous as a girl
An old ridiculous woman
Forgetting
Her age and her reason
Smiling   smiling   smiling

Girl in the River

She stood knee-deep in grey mud. Water lapped to her waist. She wore an old woollen pullover and brief colourless shorts. Her face and arms were streaked with mud and bits of shining green river weed clung to her hair. She had long strong hands with fingernails painted bright coral. On the bank behind her, purple violets and irises blossomed in little clumps, and against a huge old plum tree rested a big garden fork and wheelbarrow.

She pulled the weed from the water, reaching into it up to her elbows, dragging the heavy mass against her. She held it there, squeezing out the water, and then she braced her legs in the mud and swivelled to heave it up on to the bank behind her. The stench was sickening. She kept rubbing her nose and forehead into her shoulder, then throwing back her head gulping the clear cold air above her.

Across the river, hidden by dense lupins, a man watched her. He had been watching her for weeks. He had seen her scything the rank grass that reached the first branches of the plum tree. Clumsily at first, wielding the heavy wooden handle with chopping strokes and then gradually getting the rhythm of it and swinging the curved blade. He saw her mow the stubble so that, from the plum tree at the edge of the river, there was a stretch of smooth unbroken green up to the cottage. She planted orange and lemon trees, and silver birches and wattles and nectarines and apples. She grew flaxes and toi tois down by the river, and in the little dips and hollows of the bank she put the violets and irises. He saw her long arms and legs turn gold in the sun and her hair burn.

At first the man discussed her with his wife. He spoke of the 'brazen bitch across the river going about half-naked'. His wife went down to the river to see for herself and was shocked and angry. She wondered if there were some way they could complain about the way the girl flaunted herself. She talked it over with friends and neighbours and took a group of them down through the garden to the river.

The girl saw them standing on the far bank in a forbidding line and for a moment she was startled, then she stood up and waved to them. They saw her long legs in the faded shorts and the shape of her breasts under the tight shirt that stopped some inches above her waist, showing the bare golden flesh. They stared at her and then they turned and filed through the lupins back to the house. She watched them, leaning against the plum tree, frowning at their retreating backs.

The women decided to sign a petition and send it to the Mayor. They strongly requested that he inform the police of the girl's shameless exposure of herself in an area where they had all lived quietly and decently for years. They mentioned her two small children. That they should be taken from her and given a chance to grow up as good citizens in a Christian atmosphere. But the Mayor didn't answer the petition and they wondered whether he had ever actually received it.

After that the women never went near the river and when they heard the girl laughing and shouting with the children they would go indoors and close the windows.

The river was small and slow moving, so that logs and branches and discarded plastic containers got caught in the strong weed and stayed there lining the banks. The summer had been long and the water dropped several feet. The branches and weeds trapped the water at the river's edge and turned it stagnant and sour. The winter was cold but it brought little rain and the girl hated the still, stinking mess below the bank. She would stand under the plum tree watching the growing tangle encroaching a little further into the stream and one spring day she brought the wheelbarrow and the fork down to the bank.

The man watched her step down into the water. Her summer skin had paled but the long legs and high breasts were still as arrogant as ever. He saw her cringe as her feet sank in the soft mud.

Downstream a dozen or so mallard ducks observed her. She and the children had been feeding them for months and now they swam closer, quack-chattering hopefully for stale bread. She smiled at them and the man in the lupins heard her talking and swearing happily at them as she plunged bright painted nails into the river weed. The cold water didn't worry her. After a long time he could see the sweat gleaming on her forehead and the pile of weed on the bank grew so high she had to start another.

The children played behind her on the long sloping

lawn. Now and then they came to watch and they poked the pile of weed with enquiring fingers. 'Don't touch it,' she warned. 'It stinks.'

Around midday she climbed out of the water and went up to the cottage with the children.

The man rose from the lupins and groaned with pain. The knees of his trousers were wet and his face and hands were blue with cold.

His wife had prepared lunch and when he came inside she stared at him.

'Good God, are you ill?' she asked.

He shook his head without looking at her.

'I've been weeding.'

'Well, don't do any more — you look dreadful.' She served him hot soup and watched him with concern. The soup warmed him and his hands stopped trembling. After lunch, his wife said, 'I'm going over to Doreen's. I wish you'd come with me — you haven't seen the kiddies for ages.'

'No,' he said, 'you go on over. I'll see them at the weekend.'

'Well then . . .' she hesitated. 'Don't go back to the garden. Stay here in the warm and watch telly.'

When he heard the car start he went through the house and watched from the window for the girl. She came out of the cottage with the children. They were playing with a big yellow ball and halfway down the lawn she drop-kicked it high in the air. They screamed and raced to catch it.

'Don't kick it down here,' she called. 'You'll lose it in the river.'

She had cleared several yards and she stood on the bank with her hands on her hips, smiling and humming her satisfaction.

At the window, the man stood with clenched hands, whispering softly and rapidly. When the girl was back in the river, he slipped out of the house and ran, crouching and crab-like, to the damp hollow in the lupins.

She moved carefully out into deeper water, lifting each leg with difficulty from the mud. When she reached the mesh of logs and branches, the water covered her breasts. She was suddenly frightened of the oozing slime gripping her legs and in panic she lunged, kicking powerfully to release them. She fell face down into sharp twigs that ripped her face and arms. For a moment she lay there. The branches sank beneath her and the weed gripped her hands and legs. She pushed her head and shoulders back out of the water and then slammed forward in a frenzy, out into the middle of the river. The water ran smoothly about her and she floated with it, gasping and whimpering her relief. The man in the lupins rose and started forward.

She drifted limply down the stream for several yards and then she turned and swam back with long easy strokes. The children still played with the ball. She felt a great surge of joy to see them safe and laughing and unaware. She called to them and they came running, squealing their surprise and delight to see her swimming.

'Can we come in? Please? Can we come in too?' They danced about on the bank waving their arms, yelling at her.

'No! No, it's too cold — stay up there.' She blew kisses to them.

She tackled the branches and weed from midstream, completely at ease now. She pulled logs free and pushed them into the current. A tangle of weed broke away. She worked steadily, treading water, tearing the branches apart and guiding them into the stream. She loosened big clumps of weed, dragging them into the flow, swimming back again and again for more. And, finally, she was aware that the smell had gone. The water ran clear and clean past her bank. She swam up and down, searching the riverbed for snags that might give anchor to floating ribbons of weed from upstream and tossing them up on the bank.

At the moment when the girl made up her mind to brave the mud and get out of the river, the woman found her husband in the lupins. He heard her gasp and he cowered at her feet, unable to look at her. Then his head sank to the damp ground and he began to cry.

The girl pulled herself up on to the bank and lay there, exhausted. Her face was bleeding and her arms and legs were criss-crossed with scratches. Her coral nails were broken and filthy. She rolled over with an effort and saw the fork and the wheelbarrow.

'Tomorrow, I'll cart that weed away,' she said.

At the Conference

Sydney University, August 1988

In the midst
Of all the academic discourse
In language fearfully
Intelligent and intimidating
There's a lady
Knitting
Sitting there listening
Smiling
While her hands fly
In cobweb-fine cotton thread
She is knitting a cloth
For her dinner table
I take the risk
And disturb her concentration
'Excuse me,' I whisper
'How many stitches?'
Without
Taking her eyes off
The presenter of a paper
That has me totally confused
She murmurs
'Two thousand.'

She has made my day!

In a lecture room
Stacked
With literati from all over
The world
And not missing a word
She is knitting
Two thousand stitches
Into a dinner cloth

The Swans

for Jilly

Before I die
I want to see again
Something as perfect
As the sight
Of those nineteen
Black swans that flew
High against a bank
Of grey cloud turned
Silver at the edges
In the cold winter light

Their wings glittering
Their cries
Wild and lonely
Those fast dark birds
Heading south in
A long arrow
Stopped us in our tracks
And we two stood
Open-mouthed and wordless
Grounded by the glory
Of that beating flight

Remember, Jilly?
Remember?
Their wild cries
And those white white
Wingtips flashing

Ode to Jokers

I find falling in love so easy
'Cos there's thousands of beautiful guys
The world is alive with the darlings
Of every colour and size
They're there in the streets to be ogled
On foot and riding in cars
On buses and trains and on aeroplanes
In shops. At the pictures. In bars.
And oh! at the beaches in summer!
All youth and shoulders and thighs . . .
I go down there and I sit and I stare
With big dark shades on my eyes
And no-one would ever believe it
As my eyes dart about with sly stealth
They think I'm a lovely old lady —
That I'm there for the good of my health —
But I'm not . . . It's the jokers I covet
All that flesh on those beautiful bones
And the smiles and the teeth and the torsos!
And all those erogenous zones!

Right now I'm ready for action
I'm dying to fall one more time
In over my head and right into bed
With a toy boy just into his prime!
So come on you gorgeous young fullas
I'd like you to show me the way

With a boy about forty I could be quite naughty
So take me! And lead me astray . . .

I cannot of course swear to love you
To be faithful for e'er and a day
But I really am kind and will keep you in mind
If you prove that you know how to . . . play . . .
So just leave your telephone numbers
In a box you'll find as you go
And I'll give you all rings you lovely young things
And invite you all up for . . . you know . . .

The Wheelers' Jewel

When Topaz found she was pregnant she went straight down to the pie-cart and told Mr Wheeler.

'Mr Wheeler,' she said, 'you've knocked me up!'

Mr Wheeler dropped the bottle of milk he was holding and it went everywhere.

'Not now, Topaz,' he whispered, 'not here — I've got customers.'

'Where then?' asked Topaz.

Mr Wheeler looked at the customers, who were watching them curiously, then he looked down.

'I'll have to clean up this floor,' he said.

'I don't give a stuff about the floor, Mr Wheeler,' Topaz said. 'I want to talk about what's up with me!'

'Please,' begged Mr Wheeler, 'please Topaz, I'll come round tonight. Ten o'clock — soon as Arnold gets here to take over.'

'Ring Arnold now!' ordered Topaz. 'Tell him to come down now.'

'I can't — not with all these customers here. *Please* Topaz.'

'All right then,' Topaz nodded, 'but you better be there Mr Wheeler. Tonight! Ten o'clock sharp!'

Topaz caught the bus back to her bed-sitter. All the way
her stomach rumbled with hunger. As soon as she got
inside she opened a tin of baked beans, but the smell made
her throw them into the waste bucket. She put her head
down on the sink and cried.

'Baked beans are me favourite, what the hell's happening
to me?'

She put her head right under the cold tap and let the
water run all over her face. It took her breath away, but it
made her feel much better. She took her head out of the sink.

'That bastard!' she said, wiping her face on the tea
towel. 'He'll be sweating right now and he'll sweat worse
before I'm finished with him!'

She crossed the room and switched on the bedside lamp.
In the long mirror by the bed she looked at herself, running
her hands down her breasts and smoothing her flat little
belly. She flopped on the bed and began to cry again. In
the middle of her tears she saw the new love comic she had
bought on the way to the doctor's surgery. She stopped
crying and reached for it.

When she heard the doorbell, Topaz looked up in
surprise. Then she remembered. The clock said 10.15. She
put the comic under her pillow and looked in the mirror
again. 'I shoulda done me face,' she said. She reached
among a hoard of perfume bottles and chose one, splashing
it about her throat and wrists. When she opened the door
Mr Wheeler fell inside, grey-faced and trembling.

'Whatsa matter?' asked Topaz. 'You got the flu or
suppm?'

'I'm upset, naturally,' said Mr Wheeler.

'Serves ya right,' said Topaz. 'I'm two months gone, the doctor said.'

'Are you sure?' Mr Wheeler whispered.

'*Sure?*' hissed Topaz. 'Watcha mean sure? The doctor! He's sure!'

'I don't know what to do,' cried Mr Wheeler. 'I'm in despair, Topaz. Me and Phyllis —'

'I'm not innarested in anya that, Mr Wheeler. You been after me since I started at that pie-cart! Well, you got me now — right in the shit! An' you can get me out!' Topaz didn't really think he could.

'Look at me body,' she cried. 'It'll be ruined. What joker'll ever look at me again?'

'Don't cry.' Mr Wheeler patted her.

'Well, watcha gunna do?' Her voice rose to a wail.

'I'll have to tell Phyllis,' said Mr Wheeler.

'Will she divorce ya?' asked Topaz.

'What?'

Mr Wheeler reeled as though she had struck him.

'She might, when she hears about this,' said Topaz.

'Topaz, I been married to Phyllis for sixteen years.'

'Ya shoulda thought about that before then, shouldn' ya?'

Mr Wheeler glared helplessly about the room, then he sagged against the sink.

'Could I make a cuppa tea?' he begged.

'Suit yasself.' She turned her head away and stared at the wall.

Mr Wheeler set about making the tea, whistling tunelessly under his breath.

'You want a cup?' he asked.

'No — it'll make me sick,' said Topaz. 'Y'know what? I got bloody morning sickness and it's night-time! Wouldn' that turn ya right off?'

It turned Mr Wheeler so far off that he swallowed his tea in one gulp and put his cup down quickly.

'I'll have to go, Topaz,' he said. 'I swear I'll talk to Phyllis as soon as I get home. Phyllis'll know what to do.'

All the way home he wondered how he'd tell Phyllis and what Phyllis would do to him. Panic jumped about inside him like a mad frog.

When he told her, Phyllis was so quiet he thought she might be in shock.

'Phyllis? Phyl?' The frog in his chest dived into his belly and leapt about in the tea he had gulped. 'Oh my God,' he whispered, 'all this is too much for me — I feel ill . . .'

'So you ought,' said Phyllis at last, 'you dirty old man.'

'What will I do?' he pleaded. 'Please Phyl! I need guidance!'

'You need a swift chop in the balls, Bob, that's what you need.' But her tone was resigned. 'This Pearl —'

'Topaz,' he said.

'Where'd she get a name like that?'

'Her real name's Doreen but she doesn't like it.'

'Poor little bugger,' said Phyllis.

He grabbed desperately for a bit of the sympathy in her voice. 'Phyl — oh Phyl —' He reached for her hand.

'Don't touch me, Bob,' said Phyllis quietly. 'If you touch me, I swear I'll chop you.'

He dropped his hands and clasped them against his

stomach to quiet the frog. He began to rock back and
forth, making small moaning sounds.

'Shut up!' said Phyllis sharply. 'You sound like a dog.'

He shut up. But he clutched his stomach tighter and
rocked harder.

She watched him thoughtfully, probing her tongue
under her bottom dentures. It wasn't a pretty sight, but
it was a familiar one and he felt a little better for it. But
only briefly. Phyllis suddenly withdrew her tongue and the
dentures popped back into place.

'Do you want to marry her?'

'No! No! No!' he screamed, leaping from his chair.

Phyllis laughed.

'Oh Bob! She can't be that bad, surely.'

He slumped back into the chair.

'Okay —' said Phyllis, 'you'd better go to bed — I'll talk
to you tomorrow.'

'What're you going to do, Phyl?' he asked timidly.

'Go down to the pie-cart and have a talk with Arnold.'

On the way, Phyllis bought gin and tonic. She liked Arnold.
He was her friend. He had worked for Bob for years. She
got out of the car waving the bottle of gin at him. 'Close
up, Arn,' she said. 'We're going to get drunk!'

Arnold finished his orders and slammed down the
awnings.

'Nice to see you, Phyl,' he beamed. 'What are we
celebrating?' And then he saw the worry in her face. 'Phyl?'

'Arn — that girl who works here — that Pearl —'

'Topaz,' said Arnold.

'Oh, yes,' nodded Phyllis. 'She's going to have a baby, Arn. Bob's baby.'

Arnold's mouth fell open.

'Yes — I know —' Phyllis sighed. 'Pour us a couple of stiff ones, love.'

'What'll happen now, Phyl?' asked Arnold, sloshing gin into pie-cart cups.

'I was thinking of giving him to her.'

'Christ, Phyl!' He held out her drink with a shaking hand. 'What's she like, Arn?'

'Phyllis,' Arnold replied carefully, 'Topaz looks like peaches but she's a bunch of razor blades.'

'Well,' said Phyllis, downing her gin, 'that's probably what he needs — she could sharpen him up a bit.'

Arnold spread his hands. 'I don't know, Phyl — I don't know. I wouldn't wish Topaz on old Bob . . . What about you? Do you love him?'

Phyllis smiled wearily. 'Love, Arn? After sixteen years with Bob I don't know what the word means any more. Habit now, I think. Might have been different if we'd had kids . . .' She looked up at him suddenly. 'I couldn't get pregnant in sixteen years. She manages it in three months. It's a funny world, Arn, a bloody funny world . . .'

'Have another gin,' said Arnold gently.

When they'd finished the bottle, Arnold put her car keys in the till and sent her home in a taxi.

'You'll know what to do, Phyl,' he said warmly. 'I got faith in you.'

And, blind drunk in the back of the cab, Phyllis did know what to do.

Bob Wheeler didn't go to bed. He sat at the kitchen table drinking whisky and talking to the cat. The fourth whisky put his frog to sleep and he got brave.

'Listen, Vera,' he said, 'Phyl better watch her step — I been a good husband to her. We got a nice house and she's got her own car. I take her to Taupo every year. I let her go to the Melbourne Cup in 1983 — and that cost me. I never mucked around all that much — a bit of bumble-fumble here and there, but what man hasn't?'

He poured another whisky. 'And I'll tell you another thing — she thinks the sun shines out of Arnold, but the only reason he wasn't in like a big hungry labrador was because he's got a fast-eyed meter maid who keeps her tabs on him day and night!' He leaned down and stroked Vera's back. She smiled up at him then went back to sleep. 'You're a good friend, Vera,' he said.

He poured another drink and then it occurred to him that she might be thirsty. He brought milk and a saucer but the milk slopped all over the floor as he poured and it reminded him of the accident at the pie-cart and Topaz's bombshell. Straight away his frog woke up. He began to cry. He gave Vera a great kick and she leapt screaming through the open window. 'That serves you right, you bitch!' he sobbed. He got a mop and swished it about the floor. Vera poked her head back through the window and saw the milk. She eyed him warily and then she jumped down and began licking. He was filled with remorse. He got down on his knees and apologised. 'It's the state I'm in, Vera,' he said. Vera forgave him and went on lapping up the milk. He put the mop carefully down and passed out beside it.

Topaz went to bed without any tea because of the night-time morning sickness. She read two sentences of her love comic and fell fast asleep with her mouth open, snoring softly, in rhythmic little snorts. She looked like an angel.

In the morning Phyllis went to the kitchen for tea and aspirin. One eye was half open and the other quite shut so the top of her head wouldn't fly off. She fell over her husband and the mop. Once again Vera made a startled spring for the window. Phyllis held her head on and opened both eyes. Her husband didn't move. She closed her eyes again. Then she got up with an effort and swayed to the cupboard to feel for the aspirin. Behind the pain, her mind shrank to a hard little stone of dislike and it banished the last of her pity for him. She swallowed three aspirins and put the kettle on.

Topaz woke with an appetite. She poured milk on a bowl of Bixiewheats and ate while the toast cooked for poached eggs. She was halfway through finishing off a piece of sponge when she saw the tin of baked beans upside down in the waste bucket. For a few moments she stared at it, then her mouth fell open in a shrill howl and bits of passionfruit sponge flew all over the table. She huddled whimpering in the chair for a while, but she was still hungry so she cut another piece of cake. She bit into it and felt better straight away. The phone rang.

'Hullo,' said Topaz, swallowing a massive bite.

'Hullo, dear,' said Phyllis. 'This is Mrs Wheeler.'

Topaz almost dropped the phone. Then she rallied.

'Izzat so?' she countered.

'Now don't get upset, Pearl,' said Phyllis kindly. 'I want to help — I'd like to come round for a chat.'

'I'm not Pearl, I'm Topaz,' said Topaz. 'And how can you help? How can anybody help?' Her voice rose to a wail.

'Dear —'

'Don't "Dear" me!' spat Topaz. 'That bastard! Where's he?'

'Pissed as a fart on the kitchen floor,' said Phyllis coldly.

Topaz gulped with sudden respect.

'I'll be round in half an hour,' promised Phyllis.

Topaz put the dishes in the sink and cleaned up the cake crumbs. She washed her face and put on purple harem pants and a lolly-pink shirt. When she opened the door to Phyllis she looked like a flower. Phyllis gaped.

'You're beautiful!' she gasped. 'My God! What the hell were you doing — letting Bob Wheeler?'

Topaz shrugged. 'Ya better come in,' she offered reluctantly.

Phyllis sailed into the bed-sitter. There were big posters of pop stars on the walls and a shelf stacked with love comics. And perfume. Bottles of it, crammed on the dressing table.

Topaz saw Phyllis's eyes pop. 'They're presents,' she said. 'From Mr Wheeler.'

Phyllis looked at all the French labels.

' 'E gave me perfume and clothes and that.' Topaz smoothed her purple pants. 'I like nice things.'

'I can see that,' Phyllis nodded. 'If Bob Wheeler spent as

much on your back as he did on those bottles, you're not doing too badly, are you?'

'Watcha mean?' prickled Topaz.

Phyllis laughed. 'Yeah, so what?' she said. 'I've come here to try and help, love, not to pick on you. Do you want this baby?'

'Would you?' shrilled Topaz. 'If you was sixteen? Would you want a kid? What'll I do with a kid?'

'Do you want an abortion?' Phyllis had to ask.

'*No*! I can't do that! I can't! That's a mortal sin!'

Phyllis smiled warmly. 'Well then, dear . . .'

When Phyllis got home Bob was in the bath trying to ease the pain and stiffness of nine hours on the kitchen vinyl. She opened the door and walked right in. She was smiling. He lay there in the bath staring up at her. He felt a terrible fear and his little frog quietly died.

'It's all settled,' she said. 'I've fixed everything.' Her smile was dreadful.

'Phyl!' he screamed, trying to sit up. But his frog came back to life and turned into a toad which leapt to his throat and tried to choke him. He fell back into the bath.

'What's the matter?' Phyllis beamed.

'Tell me what's going to happen, Phyl?' he whispered.

'Oh, yeah, of course! She's coming here. Tomorrow. Young Pearl. She's going to live with us. For as long as she likes. And when the baby comes I'm having it. You'll have to move into the back room. I want that big sunny one for her.'

'*My bedroom?*' he choked.

'Not any more — it's Pearl's.'

'Topaz,' he whispered, 'her name's Topaz. Oh, Christ!'
Phyllis couldn't hear him. She was bustling into the big
room, intent on removing all traces of him, singing like a bird.

Ruth

She's gone
Her soul flew away
Beyond the cliff away
And away and away
She'll never be cold
The winds will caress her
She'll never be old
The waves will bless her
Only the tangible lies
In the earth
Ruth's song is high
Free
In the sky
And she'll sing
Forever

Priorities

If the bright light should fade
And I could never
Dance with words again —
What then? What then?
I'll tell you —
I would cry

If the wild joy should cease
And music become
No more than sound —
What then? What then?
God help me!
I would die

If you should turn away
And I might never
See your face again —
What then? What then?
Don't worry —
I'd survive . . .

A Wedding

In the year nineteen hundred and thirty-six, Aunty Prue married our insurance man. His name was Mr Armitage. He was an Englishman, a widower, tall and fair and always beautifully dressed in pale silk shirts and salt-and-pepper suits. He came to see us more often than his job warranted, but nobody minded because we all liked him. He was clever and kind and funny in a gentle way and he brought Cotton and me cigarette cards and paper twists of acid drops. They got married in our front room. Aunty Prue wore a honey-coloured dress and blue coat with a little feathered hat and blue shoes that hurt her. She looked plain and nice and she looked happy. Mr Armitage looked a complete stranger in a dark suit and white shirt. It was the first time we'd ever seen him in anything other than a donegal tweed.

We had no idea about him and Aunty Prue at first. We had no idea about anybody and Aunty Prue. She was nearly forty — quiet and ordinary and selfless. Not like Mama. Beautiful laughing Mama who turned men's hearts over with a look. I guess we thought it was really Mama Mr Armitage came to see. Then, when Aunty Prue told us she was going to marry him, we were shocked. She was ours — and now she was going to marry the insurance man.

'Who'll give her away?' Vanny wondered.

'What do you mean, "give her away"?' I asked.

'She has to have someone give her away at the wedding.'

I knew nothing about weddings. 'What for?'

'It's traditional,' Vanny explained. 'The bride is always given away to the groom. It's usually the father.'

'Oh, well,' I said, 'there's only Mama and Gram. It had better be Gram.'

Vanny looked pained. 'It has to be a man — you loony twit!' I quailed from her scorn. And then I thought about it.

'One of the fathers, then.'

She pursed her mouth thoughtfully, then she shook her head.

'Their wives wouldn't like it,' she said.

'But they're our fathers,' I persisted.

She nodded. 'Yes, they are,' she said, 'but this is Aunty Prue's wedding, not ours.'

I went to ask Aunty Prue who would give her away. She said Mr Green from the office. Mr Green was a small grey man with a stoop and I would much rather it had been one of our handsome fathers.

'Why can't it be a father?' I asked.

'No,' said Mama, 'that wouldn't be right. It's up to Prue to choose. And, anyway, I wouldn't know which one to ask.' Mama never did know which one to choose.

Until she was a girl of eighteen, Mama and Aunty Prue lived with their parents in the same street as the gas works. The Heron twins worked for the gas company. Every day they walked past the house and eventually they saw Mama. And they fell in love with her. And Mama fell in love with them. Both of them. They were exactly alike and she never bothered to discriminate. When she found out about Vanny they both wanted to marry her but she couldn't bear to choose. Grandfather insisted that she marry one or the other and in desperation she ran away.

Aunty Prue and the twins found her in a tiny room in the city and Aunty Prue said she would run away too, and they would find a house together. Aunty Prue was twenty-one and she had a good job, so they would manage, she said. And they did. Grandfather never forgave either of them. He forbade Gram to have anything to do with them, but when Vanny was born Gram sneaked away to the nursing home with lots of things she had been secretly making ever since Mama ran away. The Heron twins were there, both delirious, and Mama held a hand of each. In the background, Aunty Prue held Vanny. She didn't care what Grandfather thought or which twin was the father, she just held Vanny and let the love flow.

Five years later, I was born and Aunty Prue went through it all again. Mama and the Heron twins made the babies, but Aunty Prue made a home for us and filled it with comfort and love. In between me and Cotton, Grandfather died and the twins got married. They had waited a long time for Mama to make up her mind, but she never could. So they married sisters, which was the closest they could get to the relationship they had with Mama, and then they went right back to the old set-up. Mama loved them more than ever and when I was seven, Cotton was born. She is Mama's favourite. Vanny and I are both redheads like Mama, but Cotton, with her grey eyes and thick dark hair, is the image of our fathers. Vanny has always been Aunty Prue's favourite, I think, but Vanny says I am. So I guess we both are. And that's nice.

Everybody got new clothes for the wedding. Or nearly new. Vanny bought a yellow wool dress that cost her three weeks' wages. Mama couldn't decide and kept putting it off. The fathers gave her a pound note for Cotton and me and Vanny took us down to Mrs Barrett's GOOD AS NEW shop. Straight away I saw a shiny red dress and grabbed it, but Vanny hit my hands away.

'What the hell's wrong with you?' she hissed. 'You want to look like a bloody toffee apple?'

So I knew I'd have to go to the wedding looking sensible. At school I wore a sensible gym dress, a sensible cardigan and sensible shoes. And I hated the lot. Only the hard-up kids had sensible clothes. The lucky ones wore frills and bows and patent leather shoes.

'When I grow up,' I muttered, 'I'm going to wear what I like and nothing's ever going to be sensible.'

'Shut up,' Vanny breathed, 'or you'll wear your gym dress to the wedding.'

She chose a brown corduroy jacket and skirt and herded me into the cubicle. There was a cracked mirror on the wall that showed me a lopsided picture of myself, but Vanny stuck out the tip of her tongue and nodded her head happily.

'That's it!' she said. 'That's lovely!' I looked sadly in the mirror.

'I don't think I look right in this,' I said.

Vanny didn't even hear me.

'You can wear my cream blouse with it and I'll buy you new shoes and socks.'

Mrs Barrett put her head around the curtain and instantly Vanny became a countess.

'I'll take this for my sister Hazel and I'd like something as nice for Rachel.'

Mrs Barrett almost bowed. Cotton flashed her a radiant smile and Mrs Barrett beamed.

'What a lovely child Rachel is!'

She bustled away. I stared at the floor. I still wanted that red shiny dress. I felt the tears starting.

'Look happy, you stupid sheep!' whispered Vanny. 'Or I'll tell Aunty Prue you're out to spoil her wedding!'

She gave me a stinging clout over the ear and, grabbing Cotton's hand, she swept out into the shop. She came back a little later with a fluffy yellow jersey and a green plaid skirt. Mrs Barrett hovered behind her watching Cotton with melting eyes.

'Really, Vanessa — what a little princess!'

She was. I nodded at Vanny, open-mouthed in admiration.

Vanny forgot about Mrs Barrett and gave me a cross between a hug and a shove.

'You're a princess too. Now hurry up and put your other clothes on.'

All the way home Cotton danced and twirled and skipped her delight thinking about her new clothes, but I lost out, even with the new socks. I wanted the pale pink lacy ones to the knee, but Vanny shuddered and bought us both plain white ankle socks.

We had a dress rehearsal for Mama and Aunty Prue. I looked in the long mirror and it wasn't me at all. They said I was going to be a beauty. I laughed and poked my tongue at the red-haired girl in the mirror. She poked hers right back at me and her dark eyes danced.

The August days grew warmer and we were sure the sun would shine for Aunty Prue. Cotton and I could hardly wait. And then one day at school it hit me that, after the wedding, she wouldn't be living with us any more. I thought I would faint. I put my arms about my head to shut out the awful reality but it stayed and then I was sick. I went home in the headmaster's car. Mama was frantic.

'What is it? What's wrong with her? Oh!'

The headmaster couldn't tell her and I wouldn't until he had gone. When I told her, Mama leaned against the kitchen dresser and turned her face away.

'Mama?' I said anxiously. 'Mama?'

'I don't want to talk about it,' she whispered. She began to sob and it terrified me. 'Mama —'

She pushed me away.

'Go away and leave me alone!'

I went outside and sat on the back step. The wedding was no longer a joy to look forward to. It was a black shadow that would ruin all our lives. I stared at the garden without seeing it, without seeing anything but the terrible emptiness that living without Aunty Prue would bring. I was still sitting there when Cotton came around the corner of the house.

'Why are you home this early?'

'I was sick.'

'Were you?' Her small face tightened in concern. 'Shall I get Mama?'

'No, don't worry Mama. I don't think she's very well either.'

She sat down on the step beside me. After a while she slipped her arm through mine and rubbed her cheek against my shoulder.

'It's all right, Hazel,' she said. 'Vanny will be home soon.'

But Vanny came home with Aunty Prue and they were both full of excitement because Aunty Prue had the material for her wedding outfit. So I went to bed. I stayed awake till Vanny came and then I told her. She didn't say anything at first and I thought she had fallen asleep. Then she rolled out of her bed and came over to mine.

'Move over,' she said, 'and give's a hug.'

In the safety of her arms I let all the fear and pain go. She held me, rocking and murmuring sounds of comfort. It was quite a long time before I realised that she was crying too. In the morning I heard her singing in the bath. There was a note on the chair by my bed.

Hazel, you have to realise that sooner or later everything changes. Nothing stays the same even though you might think it does or hope it will. We've been lucky having Aunty Prue all our lives but now she's going to make a life of her own. We won't be happy about it but she will and that's what matters.

She's always looked after us but now we have to mind
ourselves. And Mama. We'll have to mind Mama. The
fathers will help. They're always very good. Probably
Gram will move in with us — I think Mama would like
that. Anyway, Aunty Prue won't be far away. We'll see
her often and we can have turns to go and stay.

I didn't have time to talk to you about this so I
wrote it down. And I think it's better written down
then we won't cry over it. Can you understand what
I'm trying to say? I hope so because I don't know how
else to explain. Love — Vanny.

When she came back from the bathroom, I said,
'Thanks for the note.'

She smiled. 'That's okay.'

Every night and weekend Aunty Prue shut herself in her
room and sewed. We played cards and ludo or read.
Usually one of the fathers was there and Mr Armitage, but
it was odd without Aunty Prue, even though she was only
in another room. Mr Armitage was so delighted about
marrying her, he grew handsomer by the hour. He was a
tall thin man with thick curly hair the colour of his suits
and his eyes were blue as the sky. At first, the fathers hadn't
trusted him. They thought he was after Mama. But when
they saw his blue eyes following Aunty Prue's every move,
they relaxed. Not that they understood him. How any man
could look at another woman when Mama was around
was beyond them. Especially Aunty Prue. When fate doled
out the good looks she certainly didn't do Aunty Prue any

favours. Mama got the lot. Every man ogled Mama, from college boys up. Except Mr Armitage. Aunty Prue's plain face and pale wispy hair, her plump body and legs, were only the packaging as far as he was concerned. Her light blue eyes twinkled with intelligence and her laughter was merry and innocent as Cotton's. He saw her as she really was. He saw the strength and the love and the wisdom in her and he knew he was a lucky man.

Two weeks before the wedding Vanny decided which boyfriend she'd invite and I was sick with jealousy. She had about a dozen to choose from but the only boy who fancied me was Ernest McCutcheon and I towered over him by about half a head. Secretly I longed to ask the school heart-throb because, along with the rest of the girls, I was in love with him, but I decided against it. My being in the third form and his being in the upper sixth didn't help, and there was the sad fact that he didn't know I existed.

I took my misery to Vanny but she was unmoved.

'For God's sake! You're twelve years old! Just be patient. In a few years you'll be fighting them off. And remember — it's Aunty Prue's day — pull a long face at the wedding and I'll flatten you!'

I didn't always understand Vanny.

The fathers bought Mama a green velvet dress and she was ecstatic. She tried it on for them and they could only gaze at her. She looked like a tulip on a stem. I had a sudden thought that in a few years I could very possibly look a little like that and my stomach turned right over. I stopped being jealous of Vanny having a boyfriend for the wedding right then.

Aunty Prue took the week off before the wedding and she and Mama were like giggling girls about the house. It shone as it never had before and the garden glowed with spring flowers. Gram came over every day and baked till all the tins were full and then she brought all her tins over and filled them too. On the last day she roasted a ham and Mama and Aunty Prue made sponges and little layered sandwiches which they wrapped in wet towels. I went to bed at ten but I was too excited to sleep. Vanny came home from the pictures with her favourite beau of the moment and I could hear them talking and laughing softly on the front steps. That's another thing I'll have to look forward to, I thought. I fell asleep imagining myself in Mama's green dress and pale shoes, queening on the front porch to some tall beautiful young man who could only whisper my name and cover my two hands with burning kisses.

I awoke in the early hours because somebody was moving about in the kitchen. It was Aunty Prue making a cup of tea. We lit the gas fire and pinched two biscuits from the laden tins. We didn't talk much.

I slid down on the floor at her feet and she put her arms around me. Her wispy hair bristled with curlers and her plain plump face streamed with tears.

'I love you,' I said. 'I love you more than anyone in the world.'

Later I made another pot of tea and, just when Aunty Prue was opening another biscuit tin, Cotton came padding in. We laughed and Mama called, 'What are you doing out of bed?'

Then she came into the kitchen with Vanny in her wake and I got three more cups.

We were still sitting there, talking and laughing and sipping tea when the sun came up in a great blaze on the perfect spring morning of Aunty Prue's wedding day.

Skeletons

Yes
It's tough on you
My children . . .

A friend said — Are you sure
You lot are not Italian?
Such hot-blooded
Explosiveness?
No
We're not
All races breed all kinds
Of lunacy
And it bombards us
From many sources —
Irish
Maori
English
The Montgomerys
Moorheads
The unknown Kahungunu man
McClatchie the whaler
In the Chatham Islands
And his daughter Emma
My great-grandmother
Who shut her daughter Emily
In a closet under the stairs

At the house in Greenmeadows
Till she broke and married
Hares the English labourer who
Had waited patiently for her
To give in
Or die . . .
Christ! Think of that!
And think of Harvey
Her favourite son
Who blew himself to hell
And took his young wife
On the journey . . .
Add to it the loonies
From Douglas Bridge
In County Tyrone
My father Long John who hated
Jews
Royalty
The rich
And the world —
His little sister Rachel died
At twelve years 'in an asylum'
He said and Lily — Aunty Banty —
In her green nylon raincoat
Who used the crook
Of her umbrella

To threaten all officialdom
Came here to escape
The curse
But it followed her
And she lived half her life
And all her death
Alone
In Porirua Hospital . . .

Ah!
No wonder we fight
With all that in our cupboards —
And I haven't even mentioned
The loose screws
On your father's side!

Love Poem

Yesterday
I watched you walk
Slim and neat-footed
Through the Sunday Market
Your bright clothes glowed
Golden as the leaves
At your feet and your hair
Was on fire you were happy
And happiness shines on you
Like the sun on daisies
— you lose that wariness
The watchful knowledge
Of pain

Suzy!
My first born
My April child
Wearing Autumn like a silk dress
Beautiful
At the Sunday Market

David

When you were born a big-headed
Bullet of a boy swollen and alien
After that flower that pale angel
Your sister I turned from you shocked
You were not mine — how could you be?
She was perfect my first born fragile
And delicate as shells she was all I
Could have wanted . . .

You wanted only food and
The Viyella blanket I wrapped you in
It made you sigh and burrow deep
Into sleep like a baby rabbit ugly
And content taking me and your snug
World for granted not knowing or
Caring what you looked like but giving
Me smiles of sly complicity aware that
I was slow to comprehend and that one
Day I would wake up to a love so easy
And so immense it would take my breath
Away and it stays undiminished despite
Your faults and mine and it grows
Stronger as I grow older and wraps
Around me warm like your Viyella blanket

A Domestic Incident

We were walking along Manners Street, My Love and I, on our way to the pictures, when there he was — my Ex. I hadn't seen him in years. He looked taller, bigger, more funereal than ever. In a black overcoat and black tie. Like a professional mourner. A bad omen, I thought. A very bad omen. And then I laughed. My Ex had always been a bad omen. I would shrug it off. I nudged My Love.

'Look,' I said. 'Look at this coming towards us! That's him. That's the reason the kids and I left home.'

'Well!' said My Love. 'I can't believe it! You must have been blinded by the brilliance of his mind.'

'I was,' I told him, 'and of course I married him on the rebound.'

By this time my Ex had seen us, if he hadn't before, and was making up his mind whether to cross the street or just stare straight ahead. I felt brave and a trifle brazen on My Love's arm and made the decision for him.

'Hello, Basil,' I said. 'What are you doing in the Windy City?'

'Hello, Biddy.' Ignoring my question. Just four syllables dripping hate.

'Cheer up, Basil,' I said. 'Life can't be that bad. This is Sam. My Love — and my next.'

He nodded coldly in the direction of My Love's feet.

'Who's looking after the children?'

'Since when have you started worrying about the children, Basil?' I asked. 'Not ever, that I can remember. You never took any notice of them.'

'I am their father,' he said through ice, 'and I want to know that they're safe and cared for while you're out enjoying yourself.'

'They can come to no harm, Basil,' smiled My Love. 'They're all locked away in a cupboard.'

Basil lunged away across the street snarling threats of legal action.

'Be careful, Basil,' I called after him, 'or I may send them all to you. I'd like to see how you'd manage four kids.'

My Love stared after his rigid back.

'Even on the rebound, Bid, I can't understand you marrying that.'

'He was at university — I was flattered. Me behind the counter in a sandwich shop without a brain in my head and him a student of law. Imagine it. And besides — I had been jilted by my true love at the time. So — I would marry him and be a rich lawyer's wife and live in Karori.'

'Well then — you got punished, didn't you?'

'Yes, I did. Now kiss me, and take me to the pictures.'

He pecked my nose.

'Biddy?'

'What?'

'Those four kids — they're beautiful. All of them. Especially Miss Thirteen. She's a cracker. They can't be his, Biddy! You must have strayed.'

I pecked his nose. He smelt like whipped cream on strawberries. I wanted to eat him but I forced myself to remember that it was Saturday night in the middle of Manners Mall.

'No, I didn't stray — they look like their mother. And don't call her "Miss Thirteen", Sam — call her Jessy.'

He pulled a face.

'That's what *you* call her.'

'I shouldn't then. And I won't any more.'

But I knew I would. When I saw her looking at us with cold resentment, when I had to be on the defensive with her, she was 'Miss Thirteen' all right. 'Sam, I'm touchy about her. I know, and I'm sorry. And I know she gives you a hard time, but she's only a little girl.'

'No, she's not, Bid. In a few months you're gonna have to call her "Miss Fourteen" and that's no little girl. She's a tough one. Pip and the twins — they're easy — I get along fine with them. But that one . . . She doesn't even speak to me, Bid.'

'Now you're feeling sorry for yourself.'

'I'm not!'

And then he laughed.

'I am. Ah, Biddy, we're wasting Saturday night arguing. What the hell!'

Right there, outside the Bank of New Zealand, he gave me a great hug.

'Anyway,' he said, with his face buried in my hair, 'when we've got kids of our own, it won't worry me. And just think what lookers ours will be, with a fella like me for their father, Bid.'

That plummeted through my mind like a bomb.
I pushed him away.

'Sam,' I said, 'I'm not a young woman. Thirty-five
is getting on. Four's a pretty good total — I've never
contemplated having another lot.'

'You will, my darling, you will,' he promised, tucking
my hand under his arm and setting off for the theatre with
happy strides.

In the film, Robert Redford's mouth reduced Barbra
Streisand to a quivering sigh and, in no time at all, My
Love and I felt the effect.

'Listen!' he breathed in my ear. 'We've been going
together long enough! I'm sick of things the way they are.
Tonight I sleep in your bed!'

I thought he was probably right. Up until then, there
had been twice at the beach in a borrowed car, and hasty
encounters on the sitting-room couch when the gang of
four were all safely asleep. My heart did a swallow dive to
the pit of my stomach and then swooped back up again.
My Love was absolutely right.

'Yes, Sam,' I whispered, 'yes, yes, yes.'

All the way home in the train we kept looking at each
other. My Love was thinking of things to come. And so
was I, but I was also thinking — how asleep were Miss
Thirteen and Pip and the twins? Maybe if we walked
home very slowly from the station? Or called in on the
next-doors for a cup of tea? Or both? I smiled at him. He
stroked my neck. Barbra Streisand didn't have a monopoly
on quivering sighs.

We walked from the station, but I forgot about the idea of cups of tea next door. There was a party going on. At my place. We could hear it before we turned the corner. When I opened the front door the place was jumping.

It's been a hard day's night, sang the Beatles from one of the old LPs. The room was full of bodies. Miss Thirteen's classmates, stomping their way through the floorboards. In the middle, the twins rock and rolling themselves to death, and Pip crouched on the hearth being Ringo, with two kitchen knives on the coal-scuttle. All around the room there were bottles of Coke and saucers of peanuts and chippies.

'Who told you you could have a party?' I yelled. 'And where'd you get the cash for all these goodies?'

'Everyone pooled their pocket money!' she yelled back. 'And I didn't think you'd mind.'

She beamed her sunniest, prettiest smile, but things came to a halt and someone turned the stereo down.

'No, don't,' said My Love. 'It's all right, keep going.'

She turned to him still smiling, and my heart leapt. Then her face closed.

'No,' she said, 'it's finished. Everybody go home.'

I saw My Love's happy grin fade.

'You little bitch! Why did you do that?' I whispered.

She pretended not to hear me and began herding her mates to the door.

'Hooray,' she said, 'see ya Monday.'

Pip got up with a sigh and took the knives back to the kitchen. I grabbed the twins and shoved them at My Love.

'Here, Sam — throw these two into bed!' She came

back into the room and saw that I was alone. She flung her arms around me and buried her face in my neck.

'Tell me why you did it, Jess.'

'Because I want there to be just us. We don't need anyone else.'

'I do, Jess. I need Sam.'

'Why do you? Why? When it makes me so unhappy.'

'Oh, Jess! I don't choose *your* friends.'

'He's not a friend! You know he's not a friend! He's all you ever think about!'

She was screaming at me and I wanted to hit her.

'Jessy,' I said, 'go to bed now. We'll talk it all out in the morning. You can sleep with me tonight and we'll fix everything tomorrow.'

How? Oh, Christ Jesus! How?

She ran from the room and I heard my door slam. Pip came ambling in for a goodnight kiss and saw my sanity sliding away. Pip, who doesn't worry much about most things, worries about me.

'It's all right, Bid. Don't take any notice of her. She thinks she can rule this house, but she can't. She's only a thirteen-year-old kid!'

'And you're an eleven-year-old one, eh?'

We grinned at each other and I hugged him.

When My Love came back I was picking up the debris. He bent to help me, white-faced and silent.

'Sam,' I begged, 'don't be hurt.'

'*Hurt*! I could kill her! Jesus, Biddy! Why does she hate me?'

'She doesn't hate you — she only thinks she does.'

'And that makes it all right does it?'

'No, Sam,' I whispered, 'it doesn't make it all right, but I don't know what to do about it.'

I put the bottles and saucers down on the hearth, and went to him.

'Come here,' I said, and drew him into my arms. I kissed and kissed his angry mouth until all the rage drained away, and the sweetness, and the beauty, and the strength, and the silk of him, held me, and melted me away, away, away.

But then the door opened and there she was.

'I can't get to sleep, Biddy,' she mumbled. 'Why don't you come to bed now?'

He moved like a snake. In a moment he was up and across the room. His hand swung back then forward to her face, whipping her head sideways as though she were a puppet.

'God damn you!' he said, in a voice I didn't know.

I came up behind him and brought my two fists down on the back of his neck. He staggered and then he turned.

'Oh, Biddy!'

But I moved past him and caught her in my arms.

'Jessy,' I whispered, 'I'm sorry. I'm so sorry, my darling.'

I rocked her in my arms, and I stroked her hair. She was shaking, but she didn't cry. He stood there staring at us. His face was grey and when he spoke his voice was husky and broken.

'Jessy? Oh, Christ! I'm sorry too. I shouldn't have done that. I'll never hit you again. Never! Biddy?'

'Get out,' I said.

'Biddy!'

'Just go, Sam.'

She was suddenly still in my arms. I put my cheek against her burning face.

'It's all right now, Jess. We'll go to bed — you and me.'

He grasped my arm but I shook him away.

'Wait,' he said. 'Listen to me. Listen. In a few years she'll be grown up. She will! And she'll go her own way. You won't stop her. And then what? What about you and me? Don't we count at all?'

'No, Sam, we don't,' I said. 'Nobody counts until she's old enough to understand. And until then there won't be anybody.'

'Do you mean that?'

He was looking at me with despairing amazement. My Love. My sweet funny Love, my bright clown. Then he was gone. I heard the door slam and his footsteps running down the path.

In my big bed, she fell asleep straight away. In my arms. For a while I lay there, and then some time later there was a thud and a cry, and a twin came blundering into the room.

'I fell out of bed! I was asleep, Biddy, and I fell out of bed! And I've *hurt* myself!'

I took one arm from around her and made a curve for him to fit in. She didn't even stir.

I lay there — warm and snug and trapped between them. And my heart broke.

From The Terrace

Once
From these windows
You could see the harbour
And ships
And seabirds
There was sunlight on the water
And a rim of hills
I loved it here
And envied you
Living in this house
The high ceilings
And the stairs
And the gleam of polished wood

But now
From all the long windows
The view
Is concrete
And glass
You are imprisoned

I could not live here
I would die in this gracious house
Shut in
By those bleak towers

Up Here on the Hill

Come on Old South Wind I yell
Do your worst
And I grin at you from these
Long windows
Here in this bright room I hold
The upper hand I say

You scream and slam and hurl
Dark rain
The trees dance and the waves come
Smashing in
The ferries bucket and twist
In the strait
And sailboards slice through the bay
Like sabres
Down on the golf course the gulls
Flock in
To sit out your rage in the bunkers
And the wild cats like drowned rats
Hunch under the lupins while

I
Glued to the window
Watching all this
My world gone mad and the noise
The noise   CRASHING

Know that you've won when
Excitement
Heady as sex
Comes swarming at me
Straight through the window glass

Wanted

I need a fella this winter
Now that the weather's turned cold
I need to be coddled this winter
'Cos I really am getting quite old

I don't want a man in the summer
I can manage quite well when it's warm
But I do need a bloke for the winter
To keep my old bones in good form

He could drive me around in a limo
On cold days of gales and rain
And keep me well fed and cozy in bed
And buy me good wine and champagne

So I'll put an ad in the paper
I'll ring up the Christchurch *Press*
I'll say that I want a nice joker
To heat up my West Coast address

Or maybe there's someone here now
Out there just listening to me
Who'd like a nice change for the winter
In my cozy wee pad by the sea

Of course he can't stay there forever
He'll have to be out by the spring
But I'll treat him right — especially at night
I'll woo him with zest and with zing!

So if he's all set for a flutter
In the coldest months of the year
If he's bored with life — fallen out with his wife
He'll have fun on the coast — never fear!

Now — if you're out there dear boys and you hear me
I'll see you right after the show
And maybe tonight we could take the first bite
Of the apple and
GO WITH THE FLOW!

The Stallion

When we moved to the house in the valley my mother said, 'Don't ever come home through the short cut, come up over the hill road.'

'Why?' I asked.

'Because of the stables. You're not to go near the stables.'

'Why?' I asked again.

'Because I said so. They're not very nice people.'

'Who aren't?'

'Stable people. They're rough and if I ever catch you coming home that way . . .' So I rode to school on the bar of my brother's bicycle and walked the long way home in the summer heat through the dust and burnt brown grass.

At the new school the teacher sat me next to Elsie O'Leary. Elsie's father owned the stables. For the first few days I was wary of her and then I forgot about it because she was nice. We walked home together as far as the turn-off and she skipped along the short-cut while I trudged up the hill. When she found out I lived a couple of hundred yards past her house, Elsie said, 'Why don't you come home through the short-cut?'

'Because I'm not allowed to,' I said uncomfortably.

'Why not? Your brother does.'

I shrugged. 'I'm just not allowed to.' And I turned up the long road.

'You're mad!' Elsie called after me.

I hunched my shoulders and made myself small in my embarrassment and shame. The metal handle of my school case grew wet and I kept changing hands and wiping the sweat down my skirt. Hating Elsie O'Leary.

My brother came home full of tales about the O'Leary boys. They could ride racehorses bareback and were all going to be jockeys when they grew up.

'Their big brother's a jockey already,' my brother said, 'and their father owns "The Shah".'

'What's "The Shah"?'

'He's the biggest, blackest horse you've ever seen and he's just like a wild beast.'

I shivered, and that night the biggest blackest horse was running through my dreams and away over the valley hills like a storm. All the next day at school I questioned Elsie O'Leary about the horse, my misery of the day before forgotten. In the end she grew impatient.

'He's just our stallion.'

'What's a stallion?'

'We breed from him.'

'What's breed?'

She scowled. 'It's putting him to the mares to get foals.'

'Foals,' I murmured. 'Baby horses.'

'Yes. You have to have a stallion to get the mares in foal.'

'Oh.' And while I was thinking about that and getting ready for another question she grinned at me, her pretty brown elf face suddenly sly.

'Do you want to see him?'

'The horse?' I whispered.

'Mmmm.'

'Where could I see him?'

'Along the short-cut.'

'He's *there*!'

'Yes. He's fenced in by the short-cut.'

'Oh, Elsie,' I breathed.

'Do you want to see him then?' Her brown eyes slanted at me — laughing and devious and foxy.

'Oh, yes! Oh, I do, Elsie!'

'But you're not allowed to take the short-cut,' she said softly.

I shuddered with excitement. 'I don't care — I'm coming.'

Walking past the turn-off I felt no guilt. I looked at Elsie O'Leary and smiled. Elsie smiled back.

My mother is wrong, I thought. She *thinks* she knows, but she doesn't.

Elsie held out a small hand and together we ran down the short-cut to the huge wooden fence.

He was standing on the far side of the enclosure, whinnying to the mares. Bigger, blacker than in my dreams. Wilder and lovelier and more fearsome than anything I had ever seen.

I stared and stared.

'Elsie,' I breathed, 'have you ever touched him.'

'Touched him!' she blinked at me. ' 'Course I haven't! Nobody can touch him except Dad and my big brother!'

'Elsie, are you very frightened of him?'

'I'm scared stiff!' she muttered.

'I'm not,' I said softly.

'I'll bet you are! Everybody is — even Dad sometimes. Only my big brother isn't.'

'If I got in the paddock would he kill me?'

'He'd smash you to bits!'

'With his hooves?'

'Yes!' She was staring at me.

'I'm still not frightened of him.'

She caught my arm tightly. 'You're not going in there though, are you?'

'No!' I shook her hand away. 'But I'm going to stick my neck through.'

'No! Don't put your neck through!' She grabbed at me. 'Oh, God! I'll get murdered for this,' she whimpered. But I was kneeling in the lush grass and I pushed my head under the big wooden bar at the bottom.

'Please,' Elsie moaned, 'please take your head out.'

'I won't.'

I pushed my head in further until my shoulders and chest were through. Elsie, wailing and cursing, was trying to pull me away. I kicked at her. 'Get away Elsie O'Leary!'

The stallion still called to the mares.

'You mad fool!' Elsie sobbed. 'That black devil will get you and I'll get the blame!'

I wriggled a little further under the fence.

'Hey! Black devil! Come and get me!'

The great head turned on its satin neck and the huge body was suddenly still. Then screaming and rearing and plunging he came for me. Hooves and thunder and rage.

I stayed there, half under the fence, until the noise of him, the screaming and the pounding and the terrible ragged breathing was almost above me. Then I rolled sideways and over and over away from the fence.

Elsie had gone.

I crouched in the grass and watched him. Still screaming, he flung back his giant head and lifting the glistening shoulders and forelegs he hung there for a moment and then slammed the slashing hooves down on to the heavy fence. I could see the huge eyes rolling and mad in his fury. Again and again he raked the fence, striking the broad timbers with hooves like knives.

'I love you, big black horse,' I whispered. 'I love you, I love you.'

And then somebody grabbed me by the hair and pulled me to my feet.

'What the hell are you doing? You mad little bitch!'

He hit me across the cheek and I went spinning against the fence on the other side of the short-cut.

When I turned he was talking to the stallion. Standing right against the fence, reaching through, and saying over and over, 'Easy boy — easy boy — easy now — easy . . .' and slipping through the fence smooth as a cat, stroking the taut muscled neck with sure soothing hands until the rage was stilled and the marvellous head relaxed.

He came sliding back through the fence. 'You'd better go home.'

'Yes,' I said.

'You're a little Montgomery, aren't you?'

'Yes.'

'You look like your brother.'

'Yes. And you're Elsie O'Leary's big brother.'

'How do you know that?'

'Because,' I said, 'because with the horse.'

His eyes slanted and he smiled at me.

'Go home now.'

'Yes.'

And I went running along the short-cut and began to cry. The great black horse and Elsie O'Leary's big brother and the long green grass and the clear summer sky were spinning, spinning, spinning.

When I was nearly home I fell into the cool sweet grass and cried and cried for a very long time and never knew why.

Shannagh

There's a picture
Of you in red overalls
Kneeling
On my old orange carpet
You are twelve years old
Your legs are long and
Your arms are thin
You are pale
As a Japanese doll
And your eyes are
Questioning
— you're waiting

To be fifteen
To wear op shop clothes
And hair gel and
Defy your mother
To retreat into dreams
And fall in love with
Television teenagers
Ignoring flesh
And blood boys

What happened
To my jewel
My flower

My ivory figurine kneeling
On a carpet the colour
Of sunsets?

Then the phone rings
And it's you
There on the other end of the line
And it doesn't matter
That you want to look
Like the punk girl from
The *Eastenders*
You're back again
Only different
You're fifteen all right
Refusing
To be your mother's little girl
Or mine
— she's gone
Forever and darling
— so's the old orange carpet

For Shannagh

On the radio
Beethhoven's 5th piano concerto
LOUD!
It's Julius Katchen — remember?
I told you about him —
The little man with all the hair
Wild
About his head
And the bald pate
His eyes
Short-sighted
Milky
Behind the big thick spectacles
His
Small plump hands?
Remember?

Ah! The music —
Katchen turning sound
Into champagne
Drenching me
His hands
Moving over the keys
Like water leaping
Over stones
LOUDER! LOUDER!

Turn it up!
His hands
Dancing

Then I see you my darling
I see you
In a shining dress
In a golden field
And you are the dancer!
Whirling
Bending
Moving away
Then spinning back
Laughing
Free
Your long hair flying
In the sun
There's no stopping you now!

And your love comes warm
On the wind
I breathe you in
And for a moment
The pain
Slips away . . .

Next Time Around

My elderly body has fallen from grace
It has fallen about all over the place
There are bits of it here that ought to be there
And a hell of a lot that ought not to be anywhere.
My hair has turned white — my face is now puggish
My dentures can't bite and my sex drive is sluggish . . .
Time was when all men were keener than mustard
But alas now it's years since anyone lusted
To get me alone in a fine feather bed
And rock me and lock me and beg me to wed
And indeed if they did, I could not perform
My actions at best would be only lukewarm . . .

Now I watch all young men with eyes that are sad
Recalling the days when I drove them all mad
And knowing that now I am over the hill
And with even a way, I'd not have the will . . .
I've taken to knitting, and gossip, and gin!
There's nothing else for it — I've had to give in
The curse of old age has deadened my senses
And all that was young is now in past tenses

BUT
If there is truth in reincarnation
You bet I'll be back! Come hell or damnation!
I won't make the mistakes I made in the past
I'll lead the good life and I'll live it up fast!
I'll let passion sway me to swoon and give in
To beautiful men intent upon sin
I'll quaff all the wine and I'll pluck all the fruit
And morals and virtue can go down the chute!
I had them in this life — I made them *my goal*!
And where did that get me? Down a bloody great hole!

SO BRING ON THE NEXT LIFE!
I'M READY TO R-O-O-O-L-L-L-L-L!

The Circus

One early spring night, a night of soft drifting rain and unseasonable warmth, three people were involved in an odd encounter. A middle-aged man and woman who knew each other well, or perhaps didn't know each other at all, and a stranger whom neither of them had ever seen before and never saw again.

The man's name was Jeremy Schaffer. He was fifty but could have been ten years younger. He was short and broad-shouldered, with dark bushy hair and pale blue eyes in a clever attractive face. There was an ex-wife somewhere and a couple of adult children. His present bachelor existence suited him, but it also worried him. He couldn't help the feeling that it wasn't quite proper to be unmarried at fifty. He had several woman friends. One of them was Nora Shannon. She was a big glowing woman in her forties, red-haired and dark-eyed. She was in love with Jeremy Schaffer, desperately, painfully in love, as a young girl loves.

When they met, he was attracted by things about her which later appalled him. In the beginning, he had her safely pigeonholed in his mind as a happy being, full of life, uncomplicated but exciting. He found he enjoyed her company without having to try very hard. He was more relaxed with her than with any other woman he knew.

And then he began to notice things about her which startled him and revealed that the simple genial woman he had imagined her to be, did not exist.

The truth was that when she met him, she lost her balance. She fell in love straight away. She was joyous and honest and unwary. And when it was too late, she couldn't help herself. Then, on that warm spring night, something happened to her. Nothing really changed, but things were never quite the same again.

He called for her at nine and, as usual, he was exactly on time. She often wished he might be a little late or even early, but he never was. She was ready, which wasn't usual, tall and stunning and, in those first few moments, excited and flushed as a girl at the sight of him. He never liked that in her, he felt she always did everything to excess, and his disapproval replaced the genuine feeling of pleasure at the thought of seeing her again. She saw it at once, in the tight smile, in his perfunctory greeting of her.

'Oh, Christ!' And then she leaned forward as she always did and kissed him. He felt a swift response and he pulled away a little and smiled at her. She didn't see the relaxing, the gentleness. Her eyes were glazed with tears and she turned from him. But as they drove she panicked at the silence and began to talk quickly with a prattling gaiety that horrified him.

'Guess what? I got a chain-letter today and if I don't answer it within twenty-four hours terrible things will happen to me. Mrs Someone in Timbuktoo broke the chain and dropped dead and the President of Somewhere did too and now he's no longer president. But a lowly farmhand in the Scottish Highlands did the right thing and he's made millions!'

'Are you serious?'

'What do you mean?' she asked sharply.

'Well — it all sounds like so much bullshit!'

'Of course it's bullshit! Chain-letters are bullshit! I told you about it because I thought it would amuse you.'

'Did you really get a chain-letter?'

She thought of the silly little note on her desk threatening dire misfortune if she failed to send it on. 'I'll send you a copy,' she said coldly, 'and if you don't answer it — you drop dead!'

They drove the rest of the way in silence.

The party was still in the awkward early stage. People sipped their first drinks and waited for the ice to crack. It always did when Nora arrived and, despite the misery of the car ride, she sailed into the big room with Jeremy in her wake, stopping to hug people, waving and calling to others, noticing happily the sudden ripple of pleasure at her arrival. Somebody brought them drinks and she moved easily about the room talking and laughing and already flirting with the men she knew, while their wives smiled their acceptance. They were never offended. They said Nora was too honest, too open. But she wasn't — it was simply that she didn't covet their men. Her flirting was harmless. She would have been happiest standing with Jeremy, talking with him to others, but she knew he disliked that. He circulated as she did, but from choice. Yet he was quieter than she and he sought out men he knew, chatting almost instantly about sport, although his blue eyes took in everything and in seconds he was aware of the most attractive women in the room. Two or three of them he knew intimately and he acknowledged them with quick secret half-smiles while he talked to their husbands about which side was likely to win the cricket. His interest was genuine. He liked few things better than to watch or discuss cricket or rugby with men. He could never have discussed them with women.

A couple of hours later, Nora was in full swing. Inwardly she was aware of Jeremy's every move but nobody could have guessed, Jeremy least of all. Occasionally his eyes sought hers and he felt a glow of pleasure seeing her at the centre of an attentive and admiring group. Sometimes he would go to her and for a time they would be close, but she never relaxed for long. She watched and waited for his mood to change. He felt the tension and it puzzled and annoyed him. He would make some excuse and move away from her.

After four or five gins Nora became restless. The music was a quiet background for the conversation, which was easy now and relaxed. But she had no desire for conversation, because about then her brain and her tongue fell out of step. She became a little befuddled. Nobody noticed because she took pains to hide it. Her dark eyes widened and her voice softened to a husky drawl. Actually, at that stage, her eyes tended to narrow and her tongue to thicken. The mental and physical effort to prevent such a betrayal was difficult to summon, but years of practice prevailed. She stopped circulating and sought out a comfortable chair to curl up in, feeling sleepy and ready to go home. From across the room, Jeremy watched her and thought how relaxed and lovely she looked. He wanted to take her home and make love to her.

The chair was very comfortable and in a few minutes Nora knew she had made a mistake. If she stayed there she would fall asleep. She stood up with an effort and crossed the room carefully through the laughter and chatter to the door. In the hall the air was cool and she breathed deeply, standing with her eyes closed, grateful for the empty darkness. When she opened them she saw a couple in each other's arms right at her feet. Had she taken another step she would have trodden on them. She smothered a tipsy laugh and swerved away to the open front door. Outside the rain fell softly and the street lights shone yellow and beckoning. She went eagerly down the steps, wide awake now, walking out into the middle of the street lifting her face to the rain.

Jeremy's car was parked in front of a big shabby house with long windows wide open to the street. Loud music beat from the windows. In the shadows of a huge leafy gum, a tall skinny boy was listening. He leaned against the trunk with closed eyes, one bare sandalled foot tapping. Inside the house a crowd of young people were dancing and Nora stopped to watch them, open-mouthed with surprise and pleasure. Jeremy found her there and watched her for a moment. Then he unlocked the car and threw her shawl and bag on to the seat.

'Nora,' he called, 'let's go home. Your things are in the car.'

She turned, smiling at him. 'Isn't it beautiful? Just

listen!' She held out both hands to him. 'Dance with me Jeremy!'

'Here? In the street?' He smiled his amusement. He felt all his inhibitions about her melt. Rain gleamed in her hair and glistened on her face. He leaned forward and touched her cheek. 'Let's go home.'

'Yes! But dance with me first.'

'No, come on — don't be silly.' He reached for her hand and kissed the palm gently. 'We're going home.'

She pulled her hand away. 'No, we're not — I want you to dance with me.'

'When we get home,' he said, moving away from her and slipping in behind the wheel of the car.

'You bastard,' she said softly. 'You narrow conservative bastard!' She turned her back on him and stared up at the windows. Music from the bright room poured all around her.

'Nora! For Christ's sake! You're not twenty-one — get in the car!'

She spun to face him, incensed, shouting . . . 'Ahhhh! You'd dance with me then! You'd stand on your bloody head if I were twenty-one!'

Jeremy folded his arms across the wheel and laid his head on them. She had shattered everything, as she always did with her crazy impulses and her mad refusal to act her age.

Then the boy stepped from the shadows of the gum tree and leapt the fence with a long bound.

'Lady! I'm twenty-one and I'd love to dance with you!' He bowed. A deep exaggerated swoop with one skinny arm flung wide, long brown wet ringlets hiding his face.

Nora stared at him. He tossed back the long hair and she gazed at the crooked smiling boy's face. 'We're wasting the music.'

She laughed.

Jeremy heard her and lifted his head. She was looking up at the boy, rocking, bubbling with laughter. He opened the door to get out, then stopped. He saw her, arms outstretched, her head thrown back like some big flamboyant bird, dancing in the rain. The boy led her. They swayed and stamped and circled, their feet shuffling, their heads dipping and shaking, leaning to each other then bending away in the amber light of the street lamp. A goose-woman and a heron-boy in a queer erotic ritual. It seemed endless. Jeremy watched them with shock and revulsion. He saw Nora's face and he hated her then. Her smile was intense and sly. The boy knew it and he wheeled around her, laughing and triumphant.

Then suddenly, it was all over. The music stopped and he saw them fall into each other's arms. Nora reached up and kissed the boy full on the mouth. He held her for a long time and then she pulled away and came to the car, sliding in beside Jeremy without looking at him or speaking.

'You bitch,' he said. 'You common bitch.'

She stared at him coldly and shrugged. He wanted to hit her hard across the mouth. Then he knew he didn't want to hit her at all. With an effort he started the car and, as they moved away, Nora turned and waved to the boy. He waved back with both skinny arms crossing and uncrossing like floppy scissors above his head until the car turned at the corner.

After a time Jeremy spoke. 'Do you want to go home?'

'Yes, I do.'

'Very well.' His voice hardened, but more than ever before he wanted to make love to her.

When they reached her flat he said, 'Goodnight Nora.' For a moment she hesitated, then she caught up her shawl and bag and got out of the car. She looked remote and calm and secretive. He was suddenly uneasy. 'Nora?'

She smiled at him and moved away.

'I'll give you a ring,' he called.

'Oh — yes . . .'

She knew he would. Tomorrow, or the next day, or the next week, he would call and she knew she would be waiting as eagerly as ever for the sound of his voice.

But for the moment, she didn't care if he did or he didn't or if she never ever saw him again — and relief flowed through her like a cool stream.

A Christmas Wish

I want a Whetton for Christmas!
Either Alan or Gary would do . . .
I'd l-o-o-o-o-ve a Whetton for Christmas
For some frolicsome festival woo
But — they tell me that Gary is married
Still . . . Alan is there to be plucked
And his eyes and his thighs are s-o-o-o-o sexy
And his body just made to be . . . admired.

I hear tell that he is a flanker?
And that sounds such a good thing to be
And his flanks and his shanks and whatever
Could certainly scrum down with me!
I want a Whetton for Christmas!
Big stocking just full to the brim
With a whopping great hunk of a flanker
Clad in nothing more than a grin!

I'd pluck him right out of the stocking
And play ball with him all Christmas Day
Then I'd urge him to score some tries on the floor
And convert them the old-fashioned way . . .
To hell with the difference in ages!
Because age does not matter at all!
O-o-o-o-h-h-hh! If I got a Whetton for Christmas!
Just imagine the rucks . . . and the mauls!

Santa — give me young Alan for Christmas —
And when you ride off on your sleigh
Reflect on the pleasure you've brought me
And heed not his cries of dismay
For I promise he won't be neglected
And before our first game's reached half-time
He'll come to see that there's much more to me
Than an elderly maker of rhyme!

A-a-a-ah-hh . . . but now the World Cup is over
And those Aussies have taken our pride
Well — I want you to know that I'm still all aglow!
That my passion has flowered! Not died!
So . . . I still want a Whetton for Christmas
And still it's that flanker I love
I don't care if the All Black selectors
Want to give him the boot and the shove!

They say he's too old for an All Black
And they say that he's had his time —
I say — What a load of old cobblers!
He's just coming into his prime!
Well — maybe not with a football — but
When it comes to the old one! two! three!
There's nobody else but young Alan
Who could get past the touchline with me!

So — I think I'll kidnap the darling
And carry him off to my lair
Where he can forget all these problems
And just be my big Teddy Bear . . .
He'll be chained to my wrist with a padlock
And he never will get away
He'll be mine! The Angel! Forever!
And Christmas will come every day!

Blatant Resistance

I have a new scarlet coat and
I look like a fire engine
And I don't give a damn
One should grow old gracefully
Somebody said — I don't know who
But I've heard it all my life and
So have you well to hell with that
I refuse to grow old any way
But reluctantly and bold as brass
And when arthritis bites in all
My bones and sleep sulks outside
My bedroom window in the dark
I just toss and turn and scratch
And swear the hours away I'm not
Growing older — it's the stupid
Betrayal of bones and flesh
That makes me feel this way but

Look at me now with springs in
My heels and the wind in my hair
Any moment I'll start whistling
And might even dance you a jig
And stop all the traffic along the
Quay wearing my new scarlet coat
And looking like a fire engine

Acknowledgements

The following poems were first published in the
New Zealand Listener:

'Wild Daisies', 'To Perth by Rail', 'Johnny Come Dancing',
'Coming Back Down to Earth', 'The Swans', 'Priorities', 'Love
Poem', 'David', 'From The Terrace', 'Up Here on the Hill',
'Shannagh', 'Blatant Resistance'.

'Ruth' was first published in *Toi Wahine: The Worlds of
Maori Women*, Eds. Kathy Irwin and Irihapeti Ramsden,
Penguin, 1995.

The short stories were first published as follows:
'Thirteenth Summer', in the *New Zealand Listener*, 1987.
'Girl in the River', in *Shirley Temple is a Wife and Mother:
    34 stories by 22 New Zealanders*. Ed. Christine Cole
    Catley, Cape Catley, 1977.
'The Wheelers' Jewel', in *Landfall 156*, 1985.
'A Wedding', in *Spiral 5*, 1982.
'A Domestic Incident', in the *New Zealand Listener*, 1986.
'The Stallion', in the *New Zealand Listener*, 1975.
'The Circus', in *Into the World of Light: An Anthology of
    Maori Writing*, Eds. Witi Ihimaera and D.S. Long,
    Heinemann, 1982.